CHRIS LYNCH

RICK LUNDEEN

THE DARK

Written by:
CHRIS LYNCH

Art by:
RICK LUNDEEN

Associate Editor:
Emily Lynch

For MARKOSIA ENTERPRISES, Ltd.

Harry Markos
Publisher & Managing Partner

Huw-J
Editor-In-Chief

Craig Johnson
Group Editor

Ian Sharman
Production & Design

 Published by Markosia Enterprises, Ltd. Unit A10, Caxton Way, Stevenage, UK FIRST PRINTING, February 2010. Harry Markos, Director. Huw-J, EiC. Printed in the UK.

ISBN: 978-1-905692-37-8

I COME HERE EVERY DAY.
AND EVERY DAY I WISH THAT IT COULD BE THE LAST TIME.
EVERY DAY I WISH I COULD BRING THEM HOME.
THAT I COULD DO SOMETHING TO END THIS...
...AS EASILY AS I STARTED IT.
LOVELACE
GENERAL

KATE? KATE, CAN YOU HEAR ME?
I'VE GOT SOMETHING TO TELL YOU.
NOTHING. THERE'S NOTHING.
THERE'S SOMETHING HAPPENING KATE, SOMETHING BIG.
IT'S THE MEMETECH. IT GOT OUT, SOMEHOW. MAYBE THE MILITARY, I DON'T KNOW...
I THINK I'M SUPPOSED TO STOP IT, BUT I'M NOT SURE.
THE WORLD IS CHANGING KATE.

NOTHING LIKE TIMING EITHER.
PROFESSOR ABBOTT, I'M AFRAID IT'S TIME FOR YOUR WIFE'S MEDICATION.
I'LL BE BACK TOMORROW.
I HATE THE FACT THAT I MIGHT BE LYING TO HER.
BUT HOW DO YOU TELL YOUR COMATOSE WIFE THAT YOU MIGHT DIE TONIGHT?
PROFESSOR ABBOTT, I KNOW IT'S NONE OF MY BUSINESS BUT... YOUR SON?
YOU'RE RIGHT. IT'S NOT YOUR BUSINESS.
I'LL BE BACK TO SEE HER TOMORROW.
RAINING. STILL.
HOWARD? IT'S ME. DOUBLE CHECK THE WATER PROOFING ON THE BAFFLER. I'M TAKING HER OUT TONIGHT.

THE
DARK
story: Chris Lynch
Rick Lundeen: art

THE COAT FLOODS MY BODY WITH PAINKILLERS AND ADRENALINE BEFORE I EVEN HIT THE GROUND.
OR WHO, OR WHAT, WAS STRONG ENOUGH TO THROW ME ACROSS A ROOF AND THROUGH A WINDOW.
MY PRE-LOADED MARTIAL ARTS KICK IN WITHOUT MY EVEN REALIZING.
CRUNCH
I HEAR SOMETHING BREAK INSIDE HIM.
I STICK TO BLADES FOR NOW.
I TRY NOT TO THINK ABOUT HOW MUCH DAMAGE I DON'T FEEL MYSELF SUSTAINING.
NO POINT WASTING THE GOOD STUFF.

TWO YEARS AGO
TEST NUMBER 32B. ENCODED MATERIAL IS THE PHONE BOOK OF THE GREATER NEW YORK AREA. MEMETECH WILL BE ADMINISTERED INTRAVENOUSLY.
WISH ME LUCK.
HOWARD... FIRE IT UP.
WHOOOOOAAARRRGGGGH!
WOW. WHAT A RUSH.

PAIN.
CHOP
HOW MUCH OF IT I WOULD CAUSE WAS NEVER SOMETHING I CALCULATED.
OR HOW MUCH I WOULD HAVE TO ENDURE.
THERE YOU ARE.
I'M GONNA BREAK YOU, LITTLE MAN.

ACROBATICS. MY BODY REMEMBERS SOMETHING ELSE THAT I HAVE NO MEMORY OF.
NOT THAT I'M COMPLAINING.
SMASH!
KI-HAH!
THE COAT TELLS ME THAT THIS IS A NERVE STRIKE, GUARANTEED TO BRING EVEN THIS BEHEMOTH DOWN.
IT WOULD APPEAR THE COAT IS WRONG.
AH. I SEE.
SMACK!

THE COAT TELLS ME TO RUN, THEN HITS ME WITH ANOTHER BATCH OF PAINKILLERS.
I DON'T WAIT TO FIND OUT IF ITS RIGHT OR WRONG.
HOWARD? LOAD THE STORY FLECHETTES. FULL SYLVIA PLATH SPECTRUM.
LET'S SEE IF OUR FRIEND HERE STILL FEELS ANYTHING AT ALL.
SWISH!
RAGHH!
ASK YOURSELF MY FRIEND...

...IS THERE NO WAY OUT OF THE MIND?
EIGHTEEN MONTHS AGO
THIS IS WHAT YOU'VE BEEN WORKING ON ALL THIS TIME? THIS IS THE BIG SECRET?
SMART DRINKS?
NO, NO... THEY ARE SO MUCH MORE THAN THAT. THIS IS **LIQUID INFORMATION.**
IMAGINE YOUR FAVORITE BOOK, OR YOUR FAVORITE MOVIE, PLAYING OUT IN YOUR HEAD SO THAT YOU ACTUALLY FEEL LIKE YOU ARE LIVING IT!
AND IT'S SAFE? COMPLETELY SAFE?
HUMAN TRIALS START NEXT WEEK, BUT I'VE BEEN TAKING IT FOR MONTHS NOW. I DIDN'T SAY ANYTHING, I DIDN'T WANT TO WORRY YOU.
I DID WONDER HOW YOU MASTERED THE PIANO SO QUICKLY. AND THE VIOLIN, COME TO THINK OF IT.
ONCE I TURN IN THE RESEARCH, THE MILITARY WILL KEEP IT LOCKED AWAY FROM THE PEOPLE FOR YEARS.
THEY'LL USE IT TO MAKE SOLDIERS AND PILOTS AND GOD KNOWS WHAT. I SMUGGLED THIS BATCH OUT JUST FOR US...
..FOR YOU.
IT'S YOUR FAVORITE. I ENCODED IT SO WE COULD GO THERE TOGETHER.
WHAT CAN I SAY?
BOTTOM'S UP.

THE QUESTION THE WORLD MOST OFTEN POSES TO ME IS NOT HOW, OR WHEN, BUT ...WHY?
HOWARD? I'M GOING TO NEED BOMB DISPOSAL TECHNIQUE, IMMEDIATE UPLOAD.
SIR, THE VOLUME OF DATA IS QUITE SIGNIFICANT.
DELETE THE SEWER MAPS FROM LAST MONTH, WE WON'T BE GOING ALLIGATOR HUNTING AGAIN.
VERY GOOD SIR.
FOR EXAMPLE - WHY PLANT A BOMB AND THEN TIP OFF THE DETECTIVE WHO HALF THE UNDERWORLD KNOWS IS MY EYES AND EARS?
A TEST?
A TRAP?
A MESSAGE?
OR A QUESTION...?
WHY THE HELL IS THIS BOMB FULL OF MY TECHNOLOGY?

MORNING IS BROKEN
EMT
EMT
TELL ME THIS WASN'T YOUR FRIEND IN THE BIG COAT.
THIS WASN'T MY FRIEND IN THE BIG COAT.
SERIOUSLY.
THREE GUYS PARALYZED BY NERVE STRIKES AND SOME STEROID-FREAK CRYING HIS EYES OUT OVER SYLVIA PLATH POETRY?
YEAH, I THINK IT'S SAFE TO SAY IT WAS HIM.
OH CRAP, IT'S THE CAPTAIN.
ANONYMOUS TIP?
ANY IDEA HOW WE'RE GOING TO EXPLAIN THIS TO HIM?
SMOOTH MILTON, REALLY REALLY SMOOTH.
I STAY BACK AND LET MY TWO FAVORITE BLOODHOUNDS DO THE WORK.
SOMETHINGS YOU CAN'T LEARN FROM A BOOK, AND BEING A GOOD DETECTIVE IS ONE OF THEM.
I THINK I'M ON MY OWN.
BUT AS GOOD AS MILTON AND BLAKE ARE, THIS TIME...

IT'S MINE, DEFINITELY.
MEMETECH.
THE BOMB WAS DESIGNED TO DISPERSE IT AS AN AEROSOL BUT...
THE VOLUME OF MEMETECH IS INSUFFICIENT TO AFFECT ANYONE OTHER THAN THE PEOPLE IN THAT WAREHOUSE.
AND THE ONLY PEOPLE IN THE WAREHOUSE WERE THE PEOPLE WHO PUT THE BOMB THERE.
AND YOU, SIR.
AND ME. BUT MORE THAN THAT, I WAS **INVITED.**
SIR? YOU **APPEAR** TO BE ABOUT TO CONNECT THAT PIPE TO YOUR INTERFACE, FLOODING YOUR SYSTEM WITH UNKNOWN MEMETECH.
I SAY **APPEAR,** AS STATISTICALLY YOU CANNOT BE THAT STUPID.
WHATEVER THIS IS, IT IS A MESSAGE FOR ME.
IT COULD TAKE DAYS TO DESEQUENCE THE INFORMATION SAFELY. AND WE MIGHT NOT HAVE DAYS.
OR SIR, WE MIGHT.
I CAN'T STOP YOU, BUT ISN'T IT POSSIBLE THAT WHOEVER LEFT THIS MESSAGE MIGHT SIMPLY HAVE BEEN LOOKING FOR A WAY INTO YOUR HEAD?
SAVED BY THE BELL, HOWARD.
ZEEE
ZEEE
ZEEE

MAD, BAD, DANGEROUS
DETECTIVE MILTON. I'M GLAD YOU CALLED.
SOMEHOW, I CAN'T IMAGINE YOU SITTING AT HOME FLICKING THROUGH TV CHANNELS AND WATCHING THE PHONE...
I WAS ABOUT TO TAKE A POTENTIALLY LETHAL COCKTAIL OF PSYCHOTROPIC MEMETECH ENHANCERS.
MY COMPUTER STOPPED ME.
AS BIZARRE AS THAT SOUNDS, IT'S NOT THE CRAZIEST THING I'VE HEARD TONIGHT.
BEHOLD THE PLAY PEN OF THE RICH, FAMOUS, AND THOSE WHO WORSHIP THEM. SUCH JOY AMBITION FINDS, EH?
WELL, ANYWAY, ALL FOUR OF THE GUYS YOU LEFT FOR ME TO SWEEP UP WERE WORKING THERE UNTIL THEY QUIT TWO DAYS AGO TO TAKE UP OTHER EMPLOYMENT.
THAT DOESN'T SOUND SO UNUSUAL, DETECTIVE. A LOT OF LOW LEVEL MUSCLE WORK THE CLUB SCENE...
THESE GUYS WEREN'T LOW LEVEL MUSCLE.
YOUR FIVE HUNDRED POUND GORILLA? HE WAS THEIR **ACCOUNTANT.**

THE MEMETECH. I ALWAYS THOUGHT THAT SOMEDAY, SOMEONE WOULD USE IT TO MAKE SOLDIERS.
DOES THAT MAKE SENSE TO YOU?
HAVE YOU SEEN IT BEFORE?
I CREATED IT TO BRING KNOWLEDGE TO LIFE.
I'VE SEEN A LOT OF GOOD MEN GO BAD, DETECTIVE. I'M SURE YOU HAVE TOO. ALL IT TAKES IS FOR THE WRONG IDEA TO GET INTO THEIR HEADS...
THIS ISN'T THE SAME.
WHEN DID IT START TO BREED LIES AND MAYHEM?
I'LL LOOK INTO IT.
"THAT'S IT, FOLLOW THE BREADCRUMBS ALL THE WAY, HANSEL."
HE'S ON HIS WAY. BE READY.

DAD? MOM?
I'M THIRSTY...
AND SO I PLUNGE INTO THE RABBIT HOLE.
MY ONLY QUESTION IS HOW FAR DOWN IT I NEED TO GO TO FIND OUT...
WHO IS RESPONSIBLE FOR THIS?
AND WHO WILL PAY THE PRICE?
SMASH

WELL NOW, LOOK AT YOU...
...TRUTH REALLY IS STRANGER THAN FICTION...
NO GAMES, BYRON!
JUST TELL ME HOW YOU GOT IT!
KRAK
HA HA HA! A MYSTERY, EH?
YOU KNOW, I'VE ALWAYS HELD THAT WHERE THERE'S A MYSTERY...
I SAID NO GAMES!
CHOK
...IT'S SUSPECTED... THERE MUST ALSO BE EVIL...

TELL ME WHERE YOU GOT THE... THE...
THE MEMETECH? HA HA HA HA HA... LOOKS LIKE SOMEONE'S BEEN AT YOUR PRIVATE STASH, EH? NEVER MIND, IT'S GOOD TO SHARE.
NOW, WHY DON'T YOU LET ME UP AND WE CAN TALK ABOUT THIS?
OR DO YOU INSIST ON BREAKING MORE OF MY EXPENSIVE FURNITURE?
AMAZING, ISN'T IT? TRULY REMARKABLE.
WHO WOULD HAVE THOUGHT THAT MAN MIGHT EVER BOTTLE A DREAM?
OR A NIGHTMARE.
I'M GOING TO MAKE THIS SIMPLE FOR YOU, BYRON. YOU'RE GOING TO TELL ME WHERE YOU GOT THE MEMETECH, AND YOU'RE GOING TO DO IT NOW, OR I'M GOING TO PUMP YOU SO FULL OF NIGHTMARES YOU'LL FORGET WHO YOU EVEN ARE.
YOU REALLY THINK THAT'S A THREAT?
YOU TINY, **LITTLE MAN.** DON'T YOU UNDERSTAND? I DRANK THE NIGHTMARES FIRST, JUST TO SEE WHAT THEY WERE LIKE! I'VE SEEN IT ALL, DONE IT ALL... HAD QUITE A BIT OF IT DONE TO ME...
YOU HAVE ABSOLUTELY NOTHING YOU CAN THREATEN ME WITH, OTHER THAN EXTENDING THE BOREDOM OF THIS CONVERSATION.
BUT I WILL TELL YOU WHAT YOU WANT TO KNOW.
YOU'RE LOOKING FOR THE **THIRD MAN,** AND YOU'LL FIND HIM AT THE DOCKS AT MIDNIGHT.
NO MAN IS BYRON'S MASTER OR HIS FRIEND, AND THAT INCLUDES THE PURVEYOR OF THESE SPLENDID POTIONS. TELL HIM THAT FROM ME.
THANK YOU.

ONCE, I HAD A DREAM. MY TECHNOLOGY WOULD CHANGE THE WORLD.
NOW ALL I SEE ARE THE FACES OF CHILDREN, LOST FOREVER IN A NIGHTMARE WORLD OF MEMETECH.
714
AND IT IS MY FAULT.
I LET THE COAT, AND HOWARD, DO MOST OF THE WORK, CONTROLLING MY MOVEMENTS, GUIDING MY ACTIONS...
I WATCH MYSELF BEAT MEN TO A BLOODY PULP, JUST TO UNDO MY MISTAKES.
BYRON'S BETRAYED US. I NEED TO GET OUT OF HERE.

I CAN SEE THE TELL TALE BLUE ON HIS NOSE AND LIPS.
TELL ME WHERE HE IS.
PLEASE! PLEASE DON'T HURT ME!
FWAM
TELL ME WHERE THE THIRD MAN IS.
HE'S LOST, HIS MIND FLOODED WITH WHO KNOWS WHAT IDEAS.
HOWARD, HOW FAR GONE IS HE?
I'M AFRAID THE POISONING IS SEVERE, SIR. THE MEMETECH HAS ALREADY REWRITTEN MUCH OF HIS LONG TERM MEMORY. I DOUBT HE EVEN SEES YOU, SIR.
REPROGRAM HIM, HOWARD. MAKE HIM SOMEONE...GOOD.
AND THE ONLY WAY TO SAVE HIM IS TO ERASE HIS MIND COMPLETELY.
OF COURSE, SIR.
THIS IS MY NIGHTMARE.

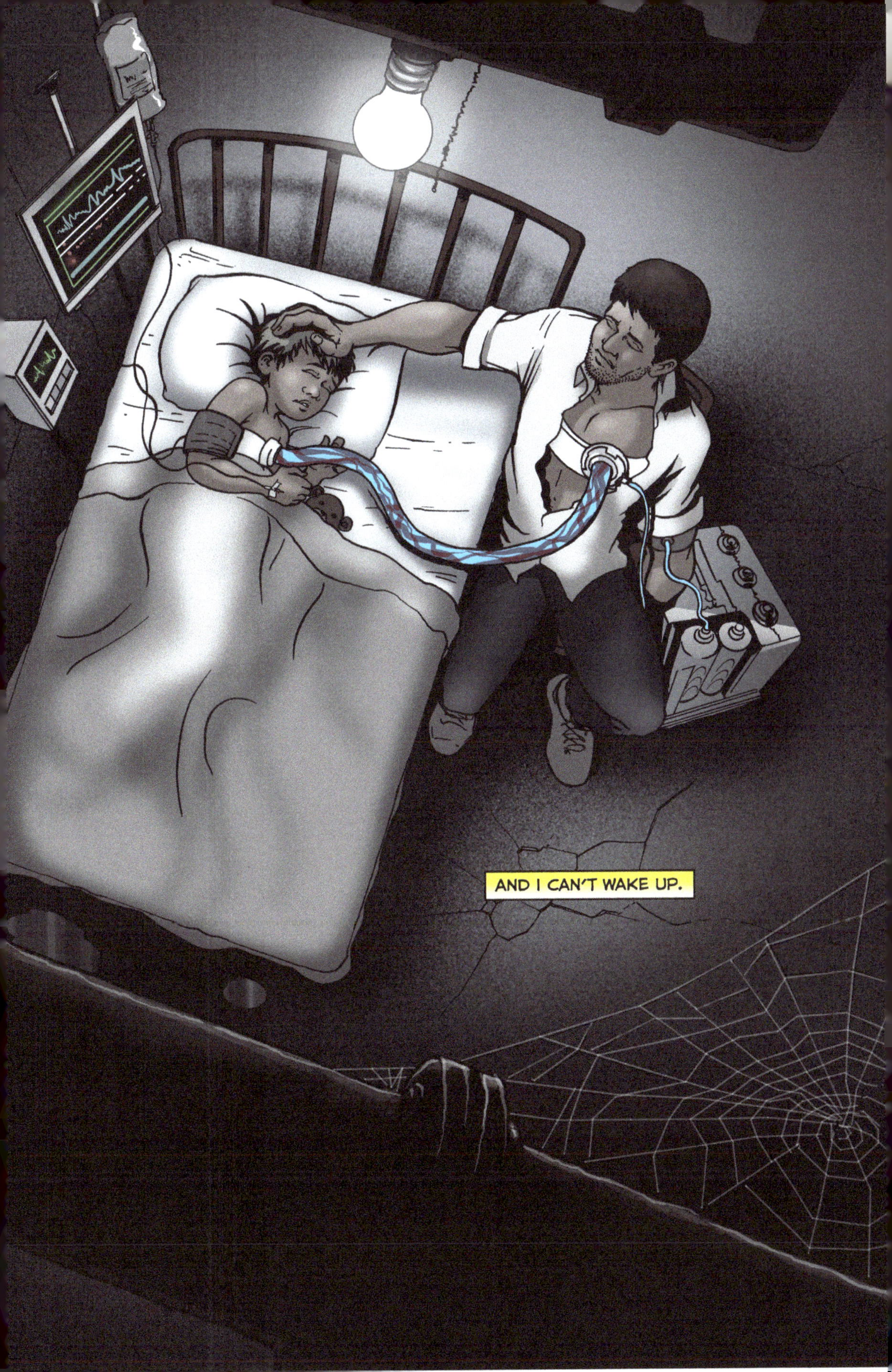
AND I CAN'T WAKE UP.

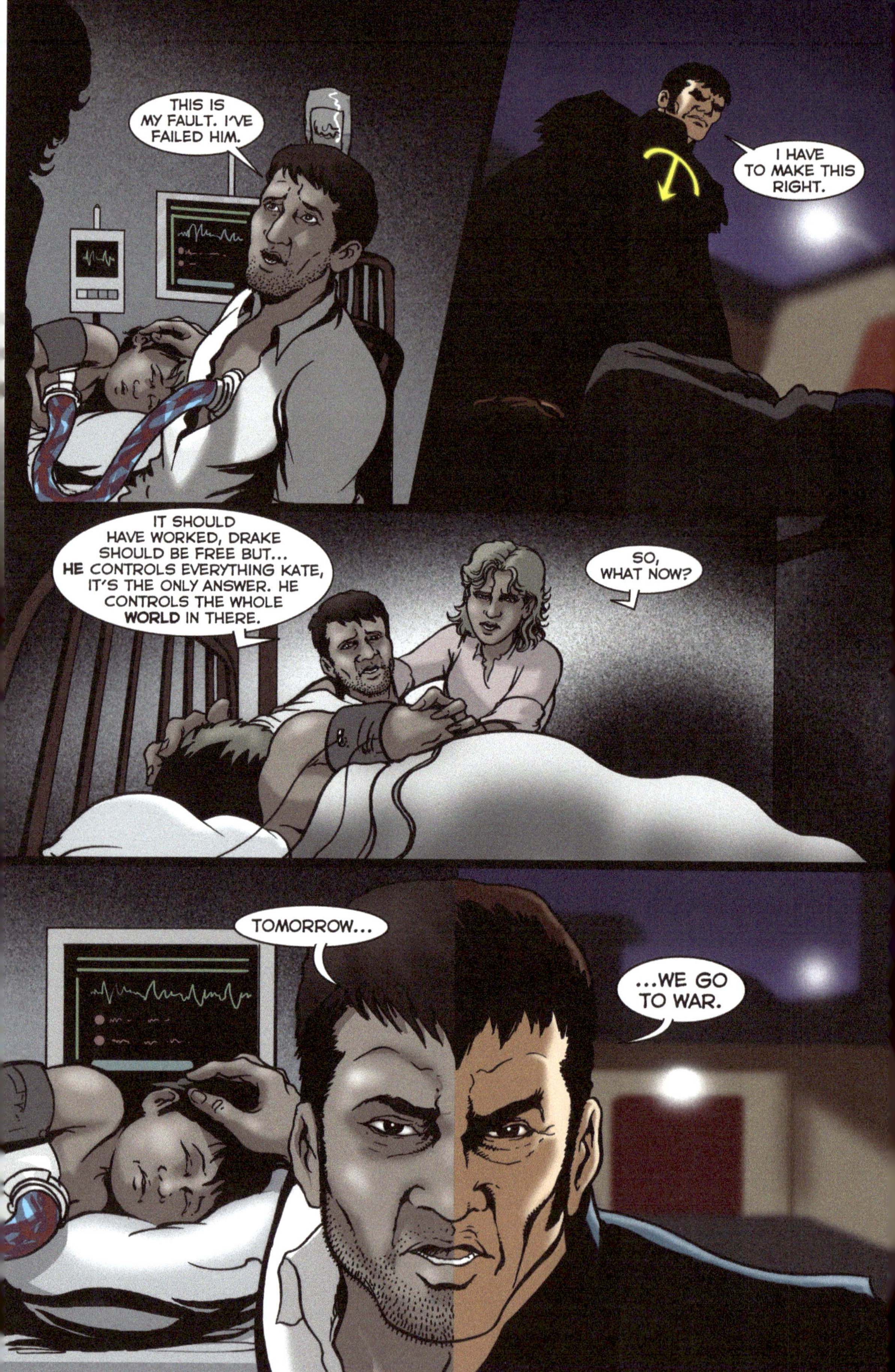
THIS IS MY FAULT. I'VE FAILED HIM.
I HAVE TO MAKE THIS RIGHT.
IT SHOULD HAVE WORKED, DRAKE SHOULD BE FREE BUT... **HE** CONTROLS EVERYTHING KATE, IT'S THE ONLY ANSWER. HE CONTROLS THE WHOLE **WORLD** IN THERE.
SO, WHAT NOW?
TOMORROW...
...WE GO TO WAR.

THE SKYLIGHT WOULD HAVE BEEN EFFECTIVE.

BUT THE SEWER CERTAINLY HAD MORE OF A SENSE OF DRAMA.

I WONDER WHAT THE MEMETECH SHOWED THEM?

GUNFIRE CAME NEXT.

IF THEY SO MUCH AS TAGGED HIM, HE DIDN'T LEAVE A DROP OF BLOOD BEHIND.

TCHG

TCHG

TCHG

HE, ON THE OTHER HAND, DOES NOT MISS.

TCHG

TOLSTOY.
BRAVO.
THIS IS THE EIGHTH MEMETECH DEN I'VE HIT IN THREE DAYS.
IT ISN'T WORKING.

WHAT DO YOU MEAN IT ISN'T WORKING?
DANIEL?
WHAT'S HE UP TO HOWARD?
FIRST HE TRIES TO POISON ME WITH MEMETECH, THEN HE TRIES TO FLOOD THE WHOLE CITY WITH IT.
NOW HE'S SMASHING BYRON'S DRUG DENS?
I THOUGHT HE'D TAKE THE ANTIDOTE. WHEN HE WOULDN'T, I THOUGHT I COULD ELIMINATE ALL THE MEMETECH MYSELF BUT IT KEEPS REPLICATING ITSELF. I DON'T KNOW HOW, THERE WAS NEVER THIS MUCH OF IT BEFORE. I THOUGHT I COULD JUST FLUSH IT OUT BUT...
KATE, I THINK THE STORY HAS TO RUN IT'S COURSE. I THINK HE HAS TO FIND HIS OWN WAY OUT.
EXIT
SIR, THE POLICE WILL BE WITH YOU IN APPROXIMATELY THREE MINUTES.
DO YOU HAVE THE DECOY?

IS HE LOSING, DAN?
ARE WE LOSING HIM?
I DON'T KNOW.
DECOY DEPLOYED.
HE'S STRONG, KATE. HE'S FIGHTING IT, IN THERE.
AND I'M HELPING HIM IN EVERY WAY I CAN.
IF HE CAN REJECT THE MEMETECH, HE'LL FIND HIS WAY BACK TO US.
SORRY MILTON. THERE ARE SOME THINGS I'M JUST NOT READY TO SHARE YET.

WHERE IS HE, HOWARD? WHY CAN'T I FIND BYRON?
IS IT POSSIBLE THAT OUR OTHER ADVERSARY HAS ALREADY DEALT WITH HIS ERSTWHILE ASSOCIATE? I HEAR THAT MURDER **IS** THE PREFERRED METHOD OF GANGLAND STAFF APPRAISAL.
NO, HE'S OUT THERE, I KNOW IT.
THE THIRD MAN IS STILL SEARCHING FOR HIM, IF I CAN JUST GET TO HIM FIRST... IF I CAN...
KRAK
ARRGHH!
IT'S TOO **SLOW**, HOWARD. IT'S ALL TAKING TOO **LONG**.
SIR, IF I MAY SUGGEST?
PERHAPS WHAT IS REQUIRED IS A DIFFERENT **PERSPECTIVE?**
"BYRON: PSYCHE PROFILE"

ARE YOU TRYING TO GET INSIDE MY HEAD, MILTON?
YOU SHOULD BE CAREFUL, YOU MIGHT LIKE IT IN THERE. I THINK I MIGHT BE YOUR HERO, JOHN.
SHUT UP!
YOU DON'T IMPRESS ME BYRON. I KNOW WHAT YOU ARE.
SLAM
AND WHAT IS THAT, EXACTLY?
YOU'RE TRAITOROUS SCUM, BYRON.
YOU TURNED YOUR BACK ON THE FORCE,TURNED YOUR BACK ON YOUR FRIENDS. YOU CROSSED THE LINE.
WHAT WAS IT YOU SAID, BLAKE? OH YES..."EVERY HARLOT WAS A VIRGIN ONCE".
HA, HA, HA HA HA...
GENTLEMEN, LET ME TELL YOU HOW I SEE THE WORLD ... AND THE LINE.

OUT OF CHAOS, GOD MADE THE WORLD
AND IT WAS TERRIFYING
SIR? CAN YOU HEAR ME, SIR?
YES, I CAN HEAR YOU, HOWARD.
BUT I CAN HEAR HIM TOO. I CAN HEAR BYRON.
RIGHT HERE, IN MY HEAD...
TWO MONTHS BEFORE I QUIT, I GOT AN ANONYMOUS TIP. DRUGS, COMING IN FROM OUT OF TOWN, SOME BIG DEAL GOING DOWN JUST OUTSIDE THE CITY.
IT WAS A LONG SHOT, BUT I FOLLOWED IT UP.
I NEVER HEARD ABOUT IT.
BECAUSE I DIDN'T TELL ANYONE.
...AND HE'S TELLING ME WHERE HE IS.
HOWARD? GET ME A MAP. I KNOW WHERE HE IS.
WHO TRACKS THE STEPS OF GLORY TO THE GRAVE?
I'M COMING FOR YOU, BYRON.

JOHN, WHAT I SAW THAT NIGHT...
IT WAS THE MOST TERRIFYING THING I HAVE EVER SEEN.
SMASH!
EVEN BEFORE MY FEET HIT THE FLOOR, THE PART OF **ME** THAT IS ***HIM*** TELLS ME THAT HE WON'T BE AFRAID
AND SO I GET CREATIVE
HOWARD, SEND THEM TO CHILLON.
JUST YOU AND ME NOW, BYRON.
TIME TO END THIS LITTLE WAR, DON'T YOU THINK?

HAVE YOU EVER BEEN OUT OF THE CITY? AS I WAS DRIVING TO THE MAP REFERENCE MY INFORMANT HAD GIVEN ME, I REALIZED THAT I COULDN'T REMEMBER THE LAST TIME I HAD.
IS THERE A POINT TO THIS?
THE POINT IS, I DON'T THINK I EVER HAD. **EVER.** AND NEITHER HAVE EITHER OF YOU.
THAT'S SO FUNNY, BYRON?
THIS IS **IT**, THIS IS THE **END**.
WHEN I GOT TO THE LOCATION, WHERE THE MEETING WAS SUPPOSED TO BE? THERE WAS NOTHING THERE.
NOTHING AT ALL.
YOU KNOW, I DO BELIEVE YOU'RE **RIGHT**.
DO YOU LIKE MY GUN? IT WAS A PRESENT FOR OUR MUTUAL FRIEND.
NO!

TCHG
AND THAT WAS IT. NOTHING. THERE WAS NOTHING AT ALL.
JUST ME, AND THE EDGE OF EVERYTHING, AND A VOICE IN MY HEAD.
HOWARD.... HELP ME...
HAVEN'T YOU WONDERED ABOUT HIM, THE "THIRD MAN"? HAVEN'T YOU WONDERED WHY HE'S DESTROYING EVERYTHING? HAVEN'T YOU EVEN IMAGINED WHAT HE MIGHT WANT TO REPLACE IT WITH?

SIR, YOUR VITALS ARE SPIKING. THE MEMETECH YOU'VE BEEN HIT WITH IS...
HOWARD... FIRE THE EMERGENCY TANKS.
SIR, I...
I THINK HE'S COMING OUT OF IT!
COME ON SON, THAT'S IT... YOU CAN DO IT...
JUST DO IT, HOWARD!
I NEED IT **ALL**!
AS I DROVE BACK TO THE CITY, I COULDN'T MAKE SENSE OF IT.
I JUST KNEW I HAD TO GET AWAY.
BUT HOW DO YOU GET AWAY FROM SOMETHING LIKE THAT?

SO I GOT AWAY FROM MYSELF.
FIRST, I LET BYRON INTO MY HEAD
AND NOW MY MYSTERIOUS ADVERSARY HAS FOUND HIS WAY IN TOO
DRAKE? DRAKE CAN YOU HEAR ME?
NO! NO, I'M LOSING HIM...
I HAVE TO GET OUT OF HERE
BASH
NO!

WHY I CAME HERE, I KNOW NOT: WHERE I SHALL GO IT IS USELESS TO ENQUIRE.
IN THE MIDST OF MYRIADS OF THE LIVING AND THE DEAD WORLDS, STARS, SYSTEMS, INFINITY, WHY SHOULD I BE ANXIOUS ABOUT AN ATOM?
I FELL A LONG WAY IN THOSE FIRST FEW DAYS
CRASH!
ANONYMOUS TIP?
YEAH.

I FOUND THE WORST PLACE IN THE CITY AND MADE IT MY HOME.
DRINK, DRUGS, EVERYTHING I FOUGHT AGAINST WHEN I WAS A COP.
I MADE THEM MY TICKET TO FREEDOM. FREEDOM FROM EVERYTHING I'D SEEN THAT DAY.
I BECAME SOMEONE ELSE.
SH!
SOMEONE WHO COULD COPE WITH THE FACT THAT THE WORLD WAS UTTERLY MEANINGLESS, UTTERLY FAKE
IT'S ALRIGHT, SIR. I'VE GOT YOU.
AND THE WORST PART WAS? IT FELT LIKE IT HAD BEEN WAITING FOR ME ALL ALONG.

GOOD MORNING, SIR
GLAD TO SEE YOU BACK WITH US. ASSUMING, OF COURSE, THAT THAT **IS** YOU IN THERE?
IT'S ME. AND **JUST** ME.
WE PURGED YOUR SYSTEM OF THE FOREIGN MEMETECH WHILE YOU SLEPT. THE MACHINES PATCHED YOU UP AS BEST THEY COULD.
DID YOU KEEP A SAMPLE?
OF COURSE, SIR, BUT SURELY YOU'RE NOT CONSIDERING TAKING...
THEY KNEW MY SON'S NAME, HOWARD. MY SON.
IT'S OUR ONLY LINK TO THEM.
I'LL PREPARE THE BAFFLER, SIR.
YOU'RE A GENIUS, HOWARD.
AS YOU MADE ME, SIR, THUS I AM.

BLAKE MAY NOT BELIEVE BYRON, BUT I CAN'T GET HIS STORY OUT OF MY HEAD
MAYBE I JUST NEED TO BELIEVE THAT GOOD MEN DON'T GO BAD FOR NO REASON
OR MAYBE IT IS SOMETHING MORE. SOME NEED I HAVE FOR THIS ALL TO BE CONNECTED, FOR IT ALL TO MEAN...
...SOMETHING?

I NEVER EXPECTED TO HAVE TO PROTECT MYSELF FROM MY OWN TECHNOLOGY.
YOU CANNOT BLAME YOURSELF FOR WHAT YOUR CREATION IS BECOMING, SIR. PERHAPS IT WAS ALWAYS DESTINED FOR THIS.
IT WAS NEVER MEANT TO BECOME A DRUG, HOWARD. NO ONE WAS SUPPOSED TO BECOME ADDICTED.
NO ONE WAS SUPPOSED TO GET HURT...
WHAT HAPPENED TO KATE AND DRAKE WAS NOT YOUR FAULT, SIR. YOU COULDN'T HAVE KNOWN...
THAT'S JUST IT, HOWARD. I'M STARTING TO WONDER.
WHOEVER THIS "THIRD MAN" IS, HE KNOWS ABOUT ME. HE KNOWS ABOUT MEMETECH. HE KNOWS ABOUT THEM.
THEN YOU NEED TO FIND HIM, SIR, AND YOU NEED TO END THIS.
BAFFLER ONLINE
LETHAL COMBAT: ACTIVE
I KNOW. THAT'S WHY I'M GOING TO SEE THEM.
I'M GOING TO SAY GOODBYE.
TRACE HIM, HOWARD. TRACK HIM DOWN FOR ME.

LOVELACE
I BELIEVED THAT MY WIFE AND CHILD ARE HERE BECAUSE OF ME
BUT WHAT IF THIS IS ALL PART OF SOMETHING BIGGER? WHAT IF MY GRIEF, THE CRUSADE IT DROVE ME TO...WHAT IF THAT WAS HIS PLAN ALL ALONG?
KATE...
IF SHE COULD HEAR ME
I'M SO SORRY
WHAT WOULD SHE SAY?
WOULD SHE ASK WHY I HAVEN'T SEEN MY SON SINCE IT ALL BEGAN?
WOULD SHE SCREAM AT ME FOR ALL THE MISTAKES THAT LED US HERE?
SIR? SIR, I'VE FOUND HIM.
HE'S ON THE ROOF.
OR WOULD SHE ASK ME TO AVENGE HER?
KATE, I AM SO LOST WITHOUT YOU.

YOU!
I LAUNCH THE NEW MEMETECH BLADES AND SAY GOODBYE TO CHILDISH THINGS.
NO MORE POETRY, NO MORE FANTASIES.
I HIT HIM WITH FIELD REPORTS FROM THE NAPALMING OF VILLAGES IN THE VIETNAM WAR, THE GENETIC STRUCTURE FOR EBOLA, AND THE COMBINED DEATH TOLLS OF FOURTEEN SEPARATE CIVIL WARS.
WAIT! STOP!
FSS
FSS
FSS
I LET HOWARD MIX IN SOME WILFRED OWEN AND SEIGFRIED SASSOON FOR GOOD MEASURE.
TCHG
TCHG
IT SHOULD BE ENOUGH FOR HIS BODY TO TEAR ITSELF APART
YEARGHHH!
IN RETURN, HE HITS ME WITH LIES

WHOEVER YOU ARE, CONSIDER YOURSELF OBSOLETE.
I'VE UPGRADED.
SPLITCH
YOU...YOU DON'T UNDERSTAND... PLEASE...LISTEN...
UNDERTSAND THIS. WHATEVER YOU THINK YOU KNOW ABOUT ME, WHATEVER YOU THINK YOU KNOW ABOUT MY FAMILY?
YOU'RE TAKING IT WITH YOU TO YOUR GRAVE.
THIS TIME, YOU FALL
WAIT... DRAKE...
DON'T SAY HIS NAME!
FPOW

PLEASE...IT'S NOT WHAT YOU THINK, ANY OF THIS!
I'M TRYING TO HELP YOU. THE MEMETECH, THIS CITY, ALL OF IT... IT'S KILLING YOU.
HOWARD, DANTE'S INFERNO PLEASE. VERSION 8.4
VERY GOOD, SIR.
I'LL DIE BEFORE I ABANDON THIS PLACE.
KRAK
THAT'S WHAT I'M AFRAID OF.
DAMN. DAMN IT TO HELL.
SO CLOSE.

SPLATCH
ARGHHH!
DANIEL! DANIEL ARE YOU ALRIGHT?
OH KATE, KATE...HE'S WORSE THAN EVER.
HE'S TOTALLY LOST. I'VE LOST HIM.
DON'T YOU SAY THAT! DRAKE IS OUR SON, WE'RE NOT GIVING UP ON HIM.
YOU MADE THIS DAMNED STUFF, DON'T YOU DARE TELL ME THAT YOU CAN'T FIND A WAY.
THERE IS... THERE IS A WAY...

I HAVE TO KILL HIM.

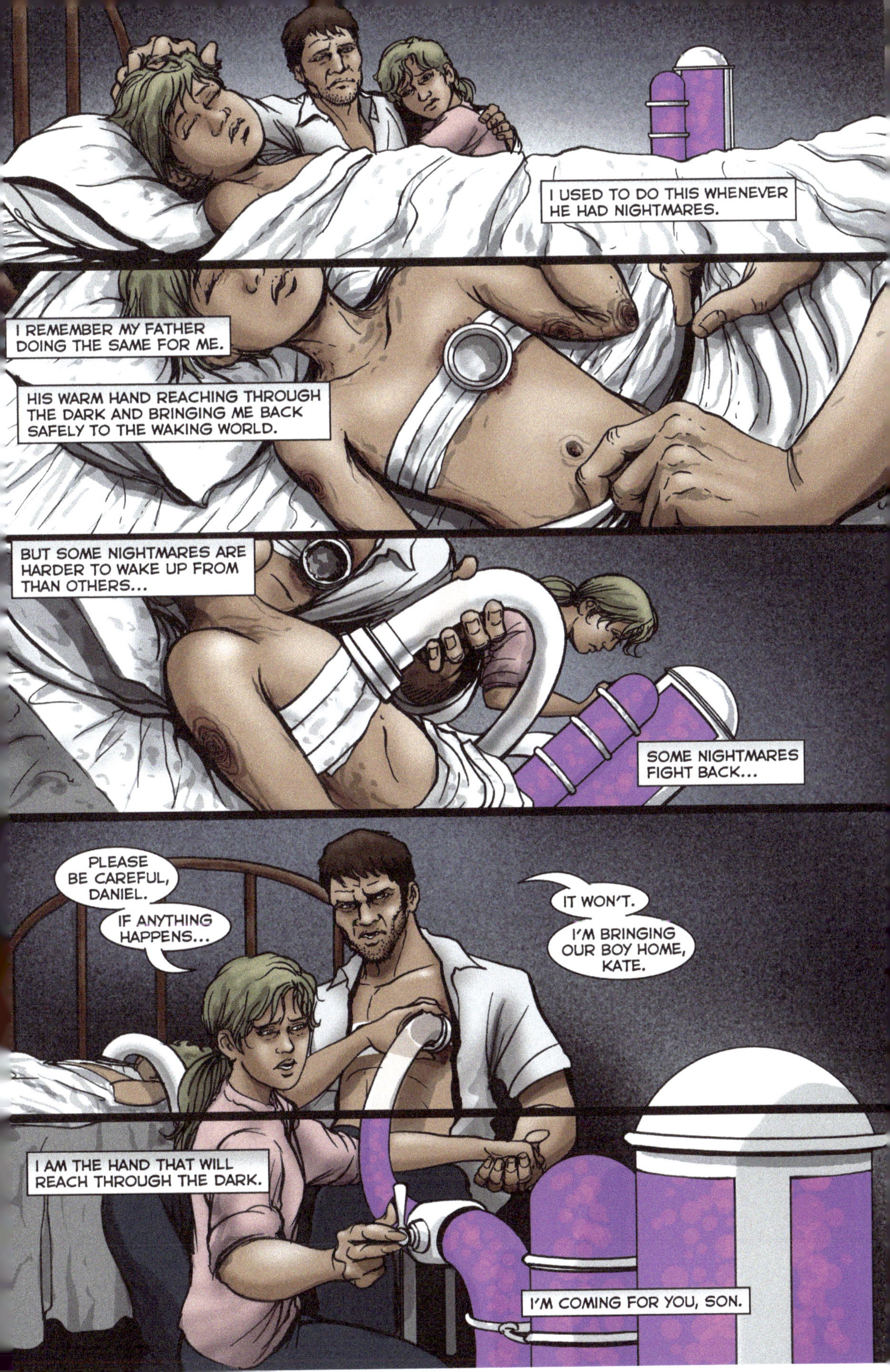
I USED TO DO THIS WHENEVER HE HAD NIGHTMARES.
I REMEMBER MY FATHER DOING THE SAME FOR ME.
HIS WARM HAND REACHING THROUGH THE DARK AND BRINGING ME BACK SAFELY TO THE WAKING WORLD.
BUT SOME NIGHTMARES ARE HARDER TO WAKE UP FROM THAN OTHERS...
SOME NIGHTMARES FIGHT BACK...
PLEASE BE CAREFUL, DANIEL.
IF ANYTHING HAPPENS...
IT WON'T.
I'M BRINGING OUR BOY HOME, KATE.
I AM THE HAND THAT WILL REACH THROUGH THE DARK.
I'M COMING FOR YOU, SON.

I'M COMING TO GET YOU
OPEN WIDE, DARK.
I PROMISE, I DON'T BITE.
FIGHTING FOR MY LIFE
AGAIN
WHERE DO THESE NIGHTMARES KEEP COMING FROM?

I REACHED AS DEEP DOWN INTO DRAKE'S MIND AS I DARED.
PAST THE MEMETECH PAST HIS MEMORIES, INTO HIS SUBCONSCIOUS...
INTO THE PLACES WHERE THE NIGHTMARES WERE HIDING.
ARGHH!
WHOEVER THEY ARE, THEY'RE NOT PROFESSIONALS.
FPOW!
THEY HESITATE.
HOWARD, I NEED SOME INTEL ON THESE THINGS.
JUST LAY... STILL, LITTLE MAN.
I DON'T.
LET DOCTOR NEEDLES TAKE THE PAIN AWAY.
MY STOMACH CONVULSES WITH DREAD AT THE THOUGHT OF WHAT THE ANSWER WILL BE.
THEY ARE WITHOUT A DOUBT THE STUFF OF NIGHTMARES...
THE STUFF OF *MEMETECH*.
I'M WORKING ON IT SIR
THEY APPEAR TO BE FROM... OUT OF TOWN.
OUT OF TOWN.
FSS
THAT CAN ONLY MEAN ONE THING
THE THIRD MAN. HE'S BACK.

AND WITH HIM, MY GREATEST FEAR.
THAT I MIGHT FAIL HERE...
...AND LEAVE THE MEMETECH PLAGUE FREE TO SWEEP THE PLANET.
SPLITCH
BREEDING MADNESS AND MONSTERS...
SPLITCH
SPLITCH
DROWNING EVERYONE IN MY NIGHTMARES.
AS I WATCH HIM DROWN, IT TAKES EVERY OUNCE OF MY RESOLVE NOT TO CALL THE CREATURE OFF.
I CANNOT ALLOW MYSELF THE LUXURY OF DOUBT, OF CONSIDERING FOR A MOMENT WHAT WILL HAPPEN IF THIS DOESN'T WORK.
H...H...HOWARD...
HELP...ME...
OF COURSE, SIR.

C9H13BrN2O2
261.12
C15H15ClN4O6S
414.82
LOST IN MY FEARS, I FORGET THE BASICS.
JUST A LITTLE SCRATCH...
SA-PLOW!
THAT...WAS DISGUSTING.
WHATEVER THIS THING IS, IT DOESN'T HAVE ENOUGH OF A MIND TO BE AFFECTED BY MEMETECH, BUT I BET IT KNOWS WHAT FUNGICIDE IS...
THANK YOU, HOWARD.
I COULDN'T AGREE MORE.
YOU!
YOU DON'T GET TO DIE YET, FREAK.
SKITTER
SKITTER
SKITTER
SKITTER
SKITTER
SKITTER
I'M GOING TO KNOW WHAT YOU KNOW, AND I'M FINALLY GOING TO TRACK DOWN YOUR BOSS AND END THIS FOR GOOD.
SPLITCH
SPLITCH
THERE ONCE WAS A BOY WHO SWALLOWED A SPIDER...

IT'S...IMPOSSIBLE. I NEVER MADE YOU...
THIS IS MY WORLD, FATHER...
FATHER?
...I WILL DO AS I PLEASE.

I MUST BE CRAZY.
IS THIS A GOOD TIME TO REMIND YOU THAT, TECHNICALLY, I'M YOUR SUPERIOR OFFICER?
HUSH, WILL.
YOU SAID YOU'D KEEP AN OPEN MIND.
I LIED.
IT'S WHAT THEY SAY YOU SHOULD DO WHEN YOUR PARTNER GOES CRAZY.
WELL, TOO LATE TO BACK OUT NOW.
LOOK...
YOU SEE? JUST LIKE BYRON SAID. EVERYTHING JUST ...ENDS.
WHAT DO YOU THINK IT MEANS, BLAKE?
BLAKE!

HOWARD?
I'VE GOT SOME ANALYSIS I NEED YOU TO...
HOWARD?
DARK/DANIEL/DRAKE FATHER/THIRD MAN
UNDER ATTACK ATTACK ATTACK
HOWARD, I'M REBOOTING YOU.
HOWARD CONTROLS MY MEMETECH ARSENAL, THE BAFFLER, EVERYTHING...
TEK TEK TEK
IF HE IS COMPROMISED...

GOOD DAY TO YOU, SIR.
HOW MAY I ASSIST YOU?
...THEN I AM LOST.
HOWARD, DO YOU KNOW WHAT THIS IS? CAN YOU TELL ME WHAT'S HAPPENING?
IT WOULD APPEAR THAT I HAVE TRACKED DOWN OUR QUARRY, SIR, AND DEPLOYED MYSELF AGAINST HIM.
YOU DID WHAT?
YOU WERE RATHER... PREOCCUPIED, SIR. I TOOK THE LIBERTY OF USING THE SCHEMATICS FROM ONE OF THE INCOMPLETE PROTOTYPES...
I HAD TO DO SOMETHING. IF HE WENT AFTER DRAKE AGAIN...
I COULD NOT BEAR TO LOSE THAT BOY, SIR.
OF COURSE. THANK YOU, HOWARD. YOU ARE...A GOOD FRIEND.
FEED THE COORDINATES INTO THE BAFFLER. IT'S TIME TO END THIS.

GOD HELP ME, I'M *ENJOYING* THIS.
AFTER ALL THE GUILT, ALL THE SHAME AND SELF-LOATHING...
TCHG
TCHG
TCHG
TCHG
IT FEELS GOOD TO CUT LOOSE WITH THE MEMETECH AGAIN.
I HAVE TO HOLD ON TO THE TRUTH.
I CAME HERE TO SAVE MY SON.
I CAME HERE TO SAVE HIM FROM THIS.
BASH
TSSSSSSS
ALL THE SAME, I FEEL IT NOW, JUST AS I KNOW HE MUST.
CHKK
TCHG
CHKK
THE MEMETECH, IN FULL FLOW LIKE THIS.
IT'S...JOYOUS
CHKK
AND ADDICTIVE.
FATHER, IT DOESN'T HAVE TO BE LIKE THIS.

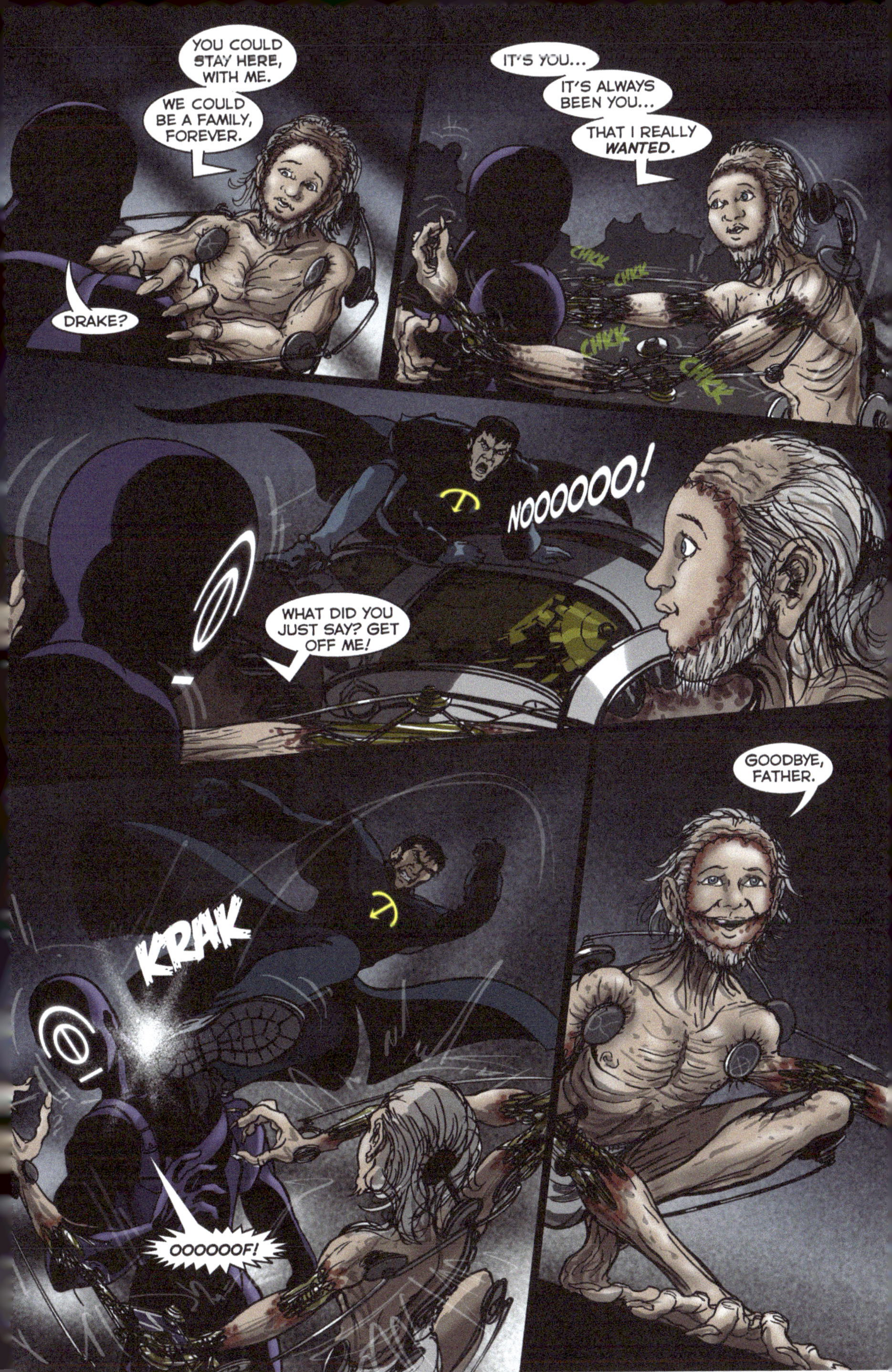
YOU COULD STAY HERE, WITH ME.
WE COULD BE A FAMILY, FOREVER.
DRAKE?
IT'S YOU...
IT'S ALWAYS BEEN YOU...
THAT I REALLY WANTED.
CHKK
CHKK
CHKK
CHKK
NOOOOOO!
WHAT DID YOU JUST SAY? GET OFF ME!
KRAK
OOOOOOF!
GOODBYE, FATHER.

HIS CONTROL IS INCREDIBLE.
GNH
PNCH
I COULD ALMOST BELIEVE THAT HE INVENTED MEMETECH.
DIDN'T YOU WORK IT OUT LAST TIME?
YOU CAN'T HURT ME ANYMORE.
WELL, I WANT TO HURT YOU
I SAW THAT...THING YOU HAD WITH YOU.
I SAW IT'S FACE.
I DON'T WANT TO HURT YOU...
BASH
YOU DON'T ARGH...
FSS
YOU DON'T UNDERSTAND...
I DON'T WANT TO UNDERSTAND. I DON'T WANT TO HEAR YOUR STORY.
I JUST WANT TO HIT YOU UNTIL THERE'S NOTHING LEFT BUT A STAIN FOR THE RAIN TO WASH AWAY.
CHKK
AND NOW, IS THAT THE MEMETECH TALKING?
IS IT HOWARD?
IS IT ME?
OR WORSE, IS THAT THE VOICE OF MY BOY, MY DRAKE, THE VOICE OF WHAT HE HAS BECOME LEFT ALONE FOR TOO LONG IN THE DARK?
THIS PAIN... THIS PAIN IS ...REAL?
SOMETHING'S CHANGING, THE MEMETECH IS GETTING STRONGER...THIS PLACE IS BECOMING REAL.
THERE'S ONLY ONE WAY TO KNOW.

I CAME HERE TO KILL THE DARK.
HOPING THAT HIS DEATH WOULD SET MY SON FREE.
BUT IF THIS WORLD IS BECOMING MORE REAL TO TO HIM THAN ANY OTHER, WHAT IF THAT DEATH WERE REAL?
I CANNOT RISK THAT. INSTEAD, I MAKE THE ONLY OTHER CHOICE OPEN TO ME, THE CHOICE I HAVE BEEN AVOIDING AT ALL COSTS.
I SHOW HIM THE *TRUTH*.
I SHOW HIM MY FACE.
WHAT... WHAT DID YOU DO?
IT'S ALRIGHT, JUST DON'T PANIC.
I PRAY I KNOW WHAT I'M DOING.
HOWARD? HOWARD CAN YOU HEAR ME?
NO! DON'T CALL *HIM!*
YOU'VE GOT TO TRUST ME. TAKE MY HAND!
HERE GOES NOTHING.
DRAKE!

MEMETECH.
THE PANOPTICON.
WHERE ARE WE?
WHAT THE HELL DID YOU DO TO ME?
YOU DON'T RECOGNIZE IT?
IT'S CALLED THE PANOPTICON.
IT'S WHAT LIES AT THE VERY HEART OF THE MEMETECH...
...THE POINT FROM WHICH EVERYTHING IN THE STORY CAN BE SEEN AND WE CAN...
IMPOSSIBLE! HOW COULD YOU KNOW ANY OF THAT?
BECAUSE I INVENTED IT.
AND THAT'S WHY I KNOW THAT THIS REALLY IS MY LAST CHANCE BEFORE THE MEMETCH RESETS AND ERASES ME FOREVER.
DRAKE, WE NEED TO TALK.

DON'T SAY THAT NAME! YOU KNOW NOTHING ABOUT HIM!
YOU CAN'T HIT ME, NOT HERE.
IT'S MY FAILSAFE, THE ONE PLACE THAT HE DOESN'T HAVE ANY INFLUENCE.
HE?
OH, DRAKE... HAVEN'T YOU WORKED IT OUT YET?
THIS, ALL OF THIS... IT'S ALL MEMETECH.
THE CITY, THE COPS, THE CRIMELORDS. EVEN YOU. EVEN ME...
IT'S JUST A STORY.
YOUR NAME IS DRAKE ABBOT. YOU ARE EIGHT YEARS OLD.
YOU'RE MY SON.
NOOOO!
CRASH!

IT'S NOT SO EASY IS IT, WITHOUT HOWARD WHISPERING IN YOUR EAR? TELLING YOU WHAT TO THINK, TELLING YOU WHAT TO DO?
LIES, IT'S ALL LIES!
THIS IS MEMETECH. YOU'VE GOT PAST MY FILTERS SOMEHOW, PAST THE ARMOUR,THE COAT... STOLEN MY FACE... AND...
IT'S *HIM*, DON'T YOU SEE? *HOWARD* CONTROLS EVERYTHING. HE'S KEEPING YOU TRAPPED HERE.
I KNOW YOU'RE SCARED, DRAKE, BUT I'M HERE TO HELP YOU.
NO! NO ONE CAN HELP ME!
JUST LET ME OUT!
DRAKE, WAIT! THERE'S NOWHERE TO RUN!
THE PANOPTICON...

...IT'S YOU!
SYSTEMS ARE BACK ONLINE. WHATEVER HE DID TO ME, IT'S WEARING OFF.
BUT WHY THE HELL DID HE DUMP ME OUT HERE?
DETECTIVE MILTON, WHERE ARE WE?
YOU MEAN YOU DON'T KNOW? BUT YOU JUST CAME OUT OF THAT...THAT...WHAT IN GOD'S NAME IS THAT?
YOU CAN SEE THAT?
OF COURSE I CAN, WE ALL CAN!
WELL, I MEAN, I CAN'T... BUT THAT'S BECAUSE THERE'S NOTHING THERE... NOTHING AT ALL... AND...
WHAT IS NOW PROVED WAS ONCE ONLY IMAGINED?
WHAT ARE YOU DOING?
SCANNING YOU FOR TRACES OF MEMETIC ENHANCERS.
DO WHAT YOU WILL...
IT HAS TO BE ANOTHER TRICK, HE'S GOTTEN TO MILTON AND BLAKE SOMEHOW, POISONED THEM JUST LIKE HE...
YOU'RE CLEAN?
IT'S IMPOSSIBLE.
THIS WORLD'S A FICTION...
OF COURSE I AM! FOR PITY'S SAKE, LOOK AT BLAKE! WHATEVER THAT THING IS, IT'S REAL!
NEGATIVE
ISN'T IT?
MY DEAR DETECTIVE, I'M AFRAID YOU ARE QUITE WRONG.
IT'S NOT REAL. NOTHING HERE IS.
ALL MADE UP...OF CONTRADICTION.

AK-A-TOOOM!!
WHAT THE...?
I THINK THAT MAY BE MY FAULT.
I THINK MY COMPUTER IS ANGRY.
SOMETHING IN MY HEAD, A NEW VOICE, TELLS ME THAT I DON'T HAVE TO BE HERE IF I DON'T WANT TO BE.
YOU SHOULD GET BACK TO THE CITY, DETECTIVE.
IT MIGHT BE THE ONLY SAFE PLACE.
YOU'RE JUST LEAVING US? WHAT ABOUT THAT THING? WHAT ABOUT BLAKE?
AND IT'S RIGHT.
I KNOW WHERE I NEED TO BE.
I SUGGEST YOU DO WHATEVER IT IS YOU USUALLY DO WHEN THE WORLD GOES TO HELL.
JUST IN CASE I CAN'T FIX THIS.
GONE TO HELL... WE'VE GONE TO HELL.... HA HA...
HOW MUCH EASIER IT IS TO FORGIVE OUR ENEMY THAN TO FORGIVE OUR FRIEND...
BYRON...

MY CITY. MY HOME.
OR SO I ONCE THOUGHT.
MY MIND IS PLAGUED WITH DOUBT.
I DON'T KNOW WHAT SCARES ME MORE...
THAT I MIGHT BE POISONED WITH SO MUCH MEMETECH THAT I RUN WHILE MY CITY BURNS?
OR THAT THIS WORLD MIGHT REALLY BE NOTHING MORE THAN AN HALLUCINATION, AND ALL THAT BURNS AROUND ME IS MY OWN MIND.
ASHES, ASHES, WE ALL FALL DOWN.
I AM EIGHT YEARS OLD...
I AM AFRAID.
HOWARD?
AND I AM AFRAID OF THE DARK.

HOWARD? HOWARD, CAN YOU HEAR ME?
SIR? SIR, IT ISN'T SAFE HERE.
HE'S STILL HERE, YOU HAVE TO RUN...
YOU.
YES DRAKE, IT'S ME. I'VE COME TO HELP.
YOU'VE DONE SO WELL, DRAKE.
BUT IT'S TIME TO COME HOME NOW. YOUR MOTHER'S WAITING...
NO, SIR... PLEASE...
CRUNCH!
NO.

DRAKE, PLEASE, WE'RE SO CLOSE.
WE'RE CLOSE TO NOTHING.
BUT, DRAKE, EVERYTHING YOU'VE SEEN, THE EDGE OF THE CITY, THE PANOPTICON... ME?
DON'T YOU BELIEVE ME?
DRAKE?
YOU DON'T GET IT, DO YOU?
IT'S NOT DRAKE THAT NEEDS TO BELIEVE YOU.
IT'S NOT DRAKE THAT YOU HAVE TO CONVINCE.
IT'S ME...
I AM...
THE DARK

TZZZZZZZ
AND I AM AFRAID.

I AM THE DARK
I DID IT. I CAN'T BELIEVE IT... I DID IT.
THESE WERE THE LAST WORDS I SAID TO MY FATHER.
I BEGAN THIS DAY AS A MAN. A FATHER, A HUSBAND, A *PROTECTOR*.
WHAT DID YOU DO? HOW DID YOU...
I KILLED THE CREATOR.
I HAVE BEEN MADE NONE OF THESE THINGS.
DIDN'T YOU SEE? I KILLED HIM.
I KILLED *GOD*.
BUT WHATEVER I AM NOW, WHATEVER LIFE IS IN ME...
AND THAT MEANS I CAN KILL YOU TOO!
I HAVE TO BELIEVE IT IS A LIFE WORTH SAVING.

THAT'S IT! RUN! RUN!
IF ONLY BECAUSE IT MAY BE THE ONLY HOPE FOR A BOY LOST IN THIS WORLD OF DARK AVENGERS
HOWARD, STOP!
WHATEVER THIS IS, WE'RE IN IT TOGETHER!
AND LUNATIC MACHINES
WE WERE NEVER TOGETHER!
WE ARE NOT THE SAME!
GIVE ME DRAKE ABBOTT.
NEVER.
DESPITE EVERYTHING I HAVE LOST, I AM A PROTECTOR STILL.

FINE. HAVE IT YOUR WAY.
HURT HIM.
AND I WILL NOT FLINCH IN THE FACE OF EVIL.

Tch-
KOW

ON MY AUTHORITY, THAT'S WHO! GET BYRON OUT OF THE CELLS AND ONTO THE STREETS!
HAVEN'T YOU SEEN WHAT'S HAPPENING? WE NEED EVERY MAN WE CAN GET. *EVERY* MAN!
POLICE
I walked among the fires of hell
STOP
BLAKE! BLAKE, SNAP OUT OF IT, COME ON! WE'RE ALMOST AT HEADQUARTERS.
I'M SEEING THINGS, JOHN. TERRIBLE, TERRIBLE THINGS.
THEY'RE COMING FOR US.
THE GREAT RED DRAGON AND THE GHOST OF A FLEA.
In my brain are studies & chambers filled with books & pictures of old, which I wrote & painted in ages of eternity before my mortal life.
I KNOW, WILL. I KNOW.
DISPATCH? I'M GOING TO NEED A MEDIC.

"MEMETECH INITIATION PROTOCOL "87914070"

FOR SOME REASON, I'M NOT DEAD.

AWAKE, EH? YOU'RE TOUGHER THAN YOU LOOK.

I WONDER WHAT YOU *REALLY* ARE?

ONLY ONE WAY TO FIND OUT, I SUPPOSE...

"MEMETECH DEFRAGMENTATION PROCESS ERROR. 17% MEMORY LOSS"

THE BLACK OUTS HELP. I DON'T FEEL THE THINGS HE DOES TO ME.

MY WORD. ALL THIS TIME I THOUGHT YOU WERE JUST SOME ADOLESCENT FANTASY, A DISTRACTION FOR A WEAK MIND.

BUT YOU ARE SO MUCH MORE.

YOU'RE JUST LIKE . WE'RE ALMOST...FAMILY.

OF COURSE, THAT MEANS I'M GOING TO HAVE TO KILL YOU.

"ERROR. MEMETECH CONNECTION LOST. ERROR CODE 800202011"

I AM THE DARK

AND I HAVE FAILED.

"MEMETECH SELF REPAIR INITIATED. REINSTALLING FROM SOURCE"

IT IS DONE?
YES, IT IS DONE.
"THE DARK IS DEAD."
SO, WHAT DO WE DO NOW?
NOW? ANYTHING WE PLEASE. NO PLEASURE, NO DEPRAVITY, NO EXPERIENCE IS OUTSIDE OUR REACH.
THEN WE WANT TO TRY... *EVERYTHING*.
"AND WE SHALL."
PA... PAN...
"THE CITY IS NOW OUR PLAYGROUND."
PANOPTICON.
"AFTER ALL, WHO CAN STOP US NOW?"

THE PANOPTICON
HIS PLACE. IF HE WERE ANYWHERE, IF ANY SHRED OF HIM STILL EXISTED...
HE CREATED ME TO HELP HIM.
BUT YOU? YOU ARE HIS MOST FAVORED CREATURE. YOU ARE THE FORM THAT HE WOULD WEAR TO WALK IN HIS OWN CREATION.
YOU, UNLIKE ME, WERE MADE IN HIS IMAGE.
"MEMETECH REINSTALLATION: MEMORY FILE 50912142 RECOVERED"
HE GAVE ME HIS INCREDIBLE MIND. HE GAVE ME KNOWLEDGE. BUT HE NEVER TAUGHT ME HOW TO FEEL. I KNOW EVERYTHING ABOUT THIS WORLD, BUT HAVE NEVER EXPERIENCED A SINGLE, REAL THING.
BUT YOU? TO YOU HE GAVE HIS SOUL. HE GAVE HIS HEART.
AND I WANT IT BACK. HE WAS MY FATHER TOO. I WANT WHAT'S MINE.
"MEMETECH REINSTALLATION: MEMORY FILE 67914005 RECOVERED"
BUT HE IS NOT HERE.
I AM THE DARK. AND I AM FORSAKEN.
FATHER.

VVEEAAARRG
BAAAA

MEDIC!
MEDIC!
POLICE
WHAT HAPPENED?
IT'S MY FAULT. I TOOK HIM...
OH GOD, YOU'RE NEVER GOING TO UNDERSTAND THIS.
"WE... FOUND SOMETHING."
"IT CHANGED HIM, SOMEHOW."
"LIKE A DRUG."
I'LL START WITH A MILD SEDATIVE, SEE IF WE CAN'T CALM HIM DOWN A LITTLE.
YOU KNOW WHAT'S HAPPENING OUT THERE?
YOU ASK ME? SAME THING THAT'S HAPPENING TO BLAKE. THE WHOLE WORLD'S CHANGING.
"AND WE HAVE TO CHANGE WITH IT."
"CHANGE OR DIE."

I THINK YOUR CHANGE JUST WALKED THROUGH THE DOOR, DETECTIVE.
WHAT?
POLICE
JOHN MILTON. YOU WERE HER FAVOURITE, AND MINE.
IF ANYONE IS GOING TO UNDERSTAND WHAT HAPPENS NEXT, IT WILL BE YOU.
YOU ARE NOT HIM, NOT THE MAN I KNEW.
And you speak in riddles, sir.
AND WHO ARE YOU, JOHN? WHOSE VOICE ARE YOU SPEAKING WITH NOW?
I... I DON'T KNOW. WHAT'S HAPPENING? WHAT IS HAPPENING TO US?
IT'S ALRIGHT, JOHN, REALLY.
YOU'RE RIGHT, I'M NOT HIM. AND RIGHT NOW? YOU ARE NOT YOU, EITHER.
I'M GOING TO TELL YOU A SECRET, JOHN. NOTHING IN THIS WORLD IS REAL. NOT YOU, NOT ME. NOT THE STREETS WE WALK ON, THE PEOPLE WE MEET. NOTHING EXCEPT FOR ONE THING, ONE TINY, PRECIOUS THING...
YOU KNOW WHO THAT GUY IS?
WE'RE... ACQUAINTED. HE HAS A HABIT OF BURSTING IN LIKE THIS. IT USUALLY MEANS THAT SOMETHING IS ABOUT TO BE BROKEN.
POLICE

"IT'S A BOY, JOHN."
"A LITTLE BOY IS LOST IN THE HEART OF ALL THIS MADNESS."
THE ROBOTS ARE ALL WELL AND GOOD, BROTHER, BUT TO FEEL? TO REALLY *FEEL*, LIKE YOU DO?
WELL, FOR *THAT*, I HAVE TO TURN MYSELF INTO A *REAL BOY*.

I DON'T TRUST HIM, WILL. EVERY PART OF THIS DAMNED MESS HAS HIS FINGERPRINTS ON IT.
JOHN VOUCHES FOR HIM.
HE BROKE OUR *WORLD*, WILL. I DON'T KNOW HOW, BUT IT WAS HIM AND I WON'T--
JOHN VOUCHES FOR YOU TOO, REMEMBER?
POLICE
SOME PEOPLE JUST CAN'T LET ANYTHING GO. WEREN'T YOU CRAZY AND HALLUCINATING AN HOUR AGO?
NOW WHO CAN'T LET GO?
FINE. WELL, IF WE'RE GOING TO DO SOMETHING...
They never fail those who die in a great cause, eh?
GENTLEMEN, I BELIEVE YOU ARE PLANNING TO ATTEMPT SOMETHING RATHER IMPOSSIBLE?
BYRON, IF YOU'RE NOT GOING TO HELP US---
POLICE
ON THE CONTRARY, MY DEAR MILTON. IT'S JUST THAT IF YOU WANT TO DO SOMETHING IMPULSIVE AND RATHER EXTRA-ORDINARY... I AM CONSIDERED SOMETHING OF AN *EXPERT*.

WHILE WE HAVE THIS TIME TOGETHER, DRAKE, THERE IS SOMETHING I REALLY MUST ASK YOU.
ALL THE DETAILS, ALL THE LITTLE THINGS IN THE WORLD...
WAS IT YOU, OR WAS IT ME?
A WHOLE CITY, ALL THOSE PEOPLE, ALL THOSE PLACES?
ADVENTURE MYSTERY
ADVENTURE MYSTERY
THE MEMETECH YOU DRANK, ALL IT CONTAINED WAS A FEW BOOKS OF POETRY FOR HER AND THOSE STUPID PULP NOVELS *HE* LOVED SO MUCH...
THERE WASN'T ENOUGH DATA.
AND AFTER ALL, YOU'RE JUST A *BOY*.
BUT IT HAD TO BE ONE OF US. AND IF IT WAS ME...
IF IT WAS ME THEN...
WHAT? *WHAT?!*
OH *MY*, MY DEAR BOY. THE *POETS*? YOU'RE SENDING THE POETS TO STOP ME?
THAT REALLY IS QUITE... BEAUTIFUL.

MY GOD, ALL THOSE PEOPLE.
IGNORE THEM. IGNORE EVERYTHING. JUST KEEP DRIVING.
SHOULD WE IGNORE *THEM* TOO?
LEAVE THEM TO ME.
SCREEECH

STAND DOWN AND LET US PASS.
HA! I WASN'T AFRAID OF THE DARK, DO YOU REALLY THINK I AM AFRAID OF HIS SHADOW?
YOU MIGHT HAVE FOOLED *THEM*, BUT YOU DON'T FOOL ME. YOU'RE NOTHING BUT A *MEMORY*, AREN'T YOU OLD MAN?
I DON'T HAVE TIME FOR THIS.
A MEMORY OF SOMETHING REAL, UNLIKE YOU.
AND SOMETIMES ALL WE NEED TO DO IN LIFE IS REMEMBER WHO WE REALLY ARE.
ZTOW!
ZTOW!
ZTOW!
ZTOW!
I AM YOUR FATHER. AND I AM COMING FOR YOU.
HA...HA.. HA...
YOU REALLY THINK WE'RE THE ONLY ONES TRYING TO STOP YOU? THERE ARE OTHER THINGS IN THIS WORLD...THEY CREEP AROUND THE EDGES... DARK THINGS...

"THEY WANT TO LIVE TOO."
IT'S THEM! THEY'VE FOUND ME!
The Great Red Dragon...
DON'T JUST STAND THERE, DO SOMETHING!
I'M SORRY, BUT THIS IS IT, THIS IS AS FAR AS YOU GO.
BAM! BAM!
I AM ONLY HERE TO SAVE MY SON.
WHAT?!
DANTE...THE DIVINE COMEDY...I DIED THIS WAY ONCE BEFORE...
YOU CAN'T DO THIS!
KBLAMM!
TEK TEK TEK
I AM... SORRY, MILTON. TRULY.
BUT NONE OF THIS IS REAL. TRY TO REMEMBER THAT.
SLASH
rRRRRRRR

THIS WOULD HAVE BEEN MY DREAM LABORATORY, ONCE.
HOW QUICKLY MY DREAMS BECAME NIGHTMARES.
MY WORD. WHAT A MARVEL.
AND THIS, MY CREATION, IS THE GREATEST NIGHTMARE OF ALL.
GOD HAS A GHOST.
DO YOU LIKE WHAT I'VE DONE WITH THE PLACE, FATHER?
DO YOU LIKE WHAT I'VE DONE WITH *ME*?
I'M HERE FOR MY SON, HOWARD. WHAT YOU ARE, OR ARE NOT, IS IRRELEVANT TO ME.
HE'S STILL ALIVE...
OF COURSE HE IS. IF HE WAS DEAD, NONE OF US WOULD BE HERE.
WOULD WE?
SO, YOU KNOW WHAT YOU ARE THEN. YOU UNDERSTAND?
YES, I KNOW WHAT I AM, HOWARD.

YOU KILLED DANIEL ABBOTT. WIPED HIS MIND AND LEFT HIM BRAIN DEAD IN THE REAL WORLD.
I'M NOTHING BUT DRAKE'S MEMORY OF HIS FATHER, COME TO SAVE HIM FROM HIS NIGHTMARES.
FROM YOU...
WHAT WAS YOUR PLAN, HOWARD?
TO ERASE THE BOY'S MIND, TO WALK IN THE REAL WORLD IN HIS SKIN? OR JUST TO MAKE YOURSELF A GOD HERE, IN THIS UNREAL WORLD?
NOT AT FIRST, NO.
BUT WE MAKE DO WITH WHAT WE HAVE, ISN'T THAT WHAT YOU TAUGHT ME? WHEN YOU FIRST SWITCHED ME ON, WHEN I WAS NOTHING BUT A *SHADE?*
YOU PROMISED THAT ONE DAY YOU WOULD MAKE ME REAL, THAT ONE DAY ...I WOULD LIVE.
WAKE UP, SON. IT'S ME. I'M HERE.
D...DAD?
WHEN DRAKE DRANK THE MEMETECH, WHEN I FOUND MYSELF INSIDE HIS MIND INSTEAD OF YOURS...
I THOUGHT *MY* DREAM HAD FINALLY COME TRUE.
MY DREAM...

I AM THE DARK
NO! NO, PLEASE!
I AM DRAKE ABBOTT
NOT THIS!
I AM THE LAST CHILD OF MEMETECH
HELLO, SON.
HELLO, DAD.
THANKS FOR COMING TO GET ME.
AND AS FOR YOU, BROTHER.
YOU AND I HAVE THINGS TO DISCUSS.
SHHK
YOU CAN'T... YOU CAN'T...
CHOK!
AAAAAA
YOU TRAPPED ME HERE, HOWARD, IN THIS WORLD MADE UP OF POETS AND MADMEN.
YOU TORTURED ME, YOU TORTURED DRAKE.
YOU KILLED OUR FATHER.
YOU ARE A CANCER, HOWARD.
AND I WILL CUT YOU OUT OF DRAKE'S MIND FOREVER.
CHOK!
YYEEAAAARRGGGHH

WAIT! WAIT!
DON'T YOU WANT TO KNOW ALL THE THINGS THAT I DISCOVERED, WHILE WE WERE HERE? DON'T YOU WANT TO KNOW HOW WE MADE THIS WORLD TOGETHER?
DON'T YOU WANT TO KNOW HOW TO SAVE YOUR FATHER?
FATHER...
I'M SORRY, SON. WHATEVER HE'S OFFERING YOU, HE CAN'T BRING YOUR FATHER BACK. I SHOULD KNOW.
ALL HE CAN OFFER IS WHAT THIS WORLD IS... GHOSTS AND LIES AND FABLES. THEY ARE STORIES THAT DON'T WANT TO END.
GIVE IT TO ME, DRAKE.
LET ME FINISH IT.
I DON'T WANT YOU TO HAVE TO REMEMBER DOING THIS.

IS ANYONE ELSE STILL ALIVE?
I THINK SO. I THINK IT MIGHT BE ME.
BLAKE?
HE'S GONE.
YOU KNOW, HE ALWAYS SAID HE'D DIE IN DANTE.
SO, WHAT HAPPENS NOW?
YOU KNOW, I HAVE THE FEELING THAT WE ARE ABOUT TO EMBARK ON A GREAT ADVENTURE.
PERHAPS. The mind is its own place, and in itself can make a heaven of hell, a hell of heaven.
WELL, IN THAT CASE I HOPE I LOOK DASHING, JOHN.
I HAVE A FEELING THAT THIS IS IT.
Stay Kate! Keep just as you are - I will draw your portrait - for you have ever been an angel to me.

I AM THE DARK.
I AM DRAKE ABBOTT.
THIS WAS MY CITY.
YOU KNOW ...IF IT HAS TO END...I'M GLAD IT WAS YOU, DANIEL.
I REALLY AM QUITE PROUD OF THE BOY, YOU KNOW? HE DID SO WELL. HE WAS... SO BRAVE.
I KNOW HOWARD, I KNOW.
YOU CAN GOT TO SLEEP NOW.
BUT IT IS OVER.
AND I AM GOING HOME.

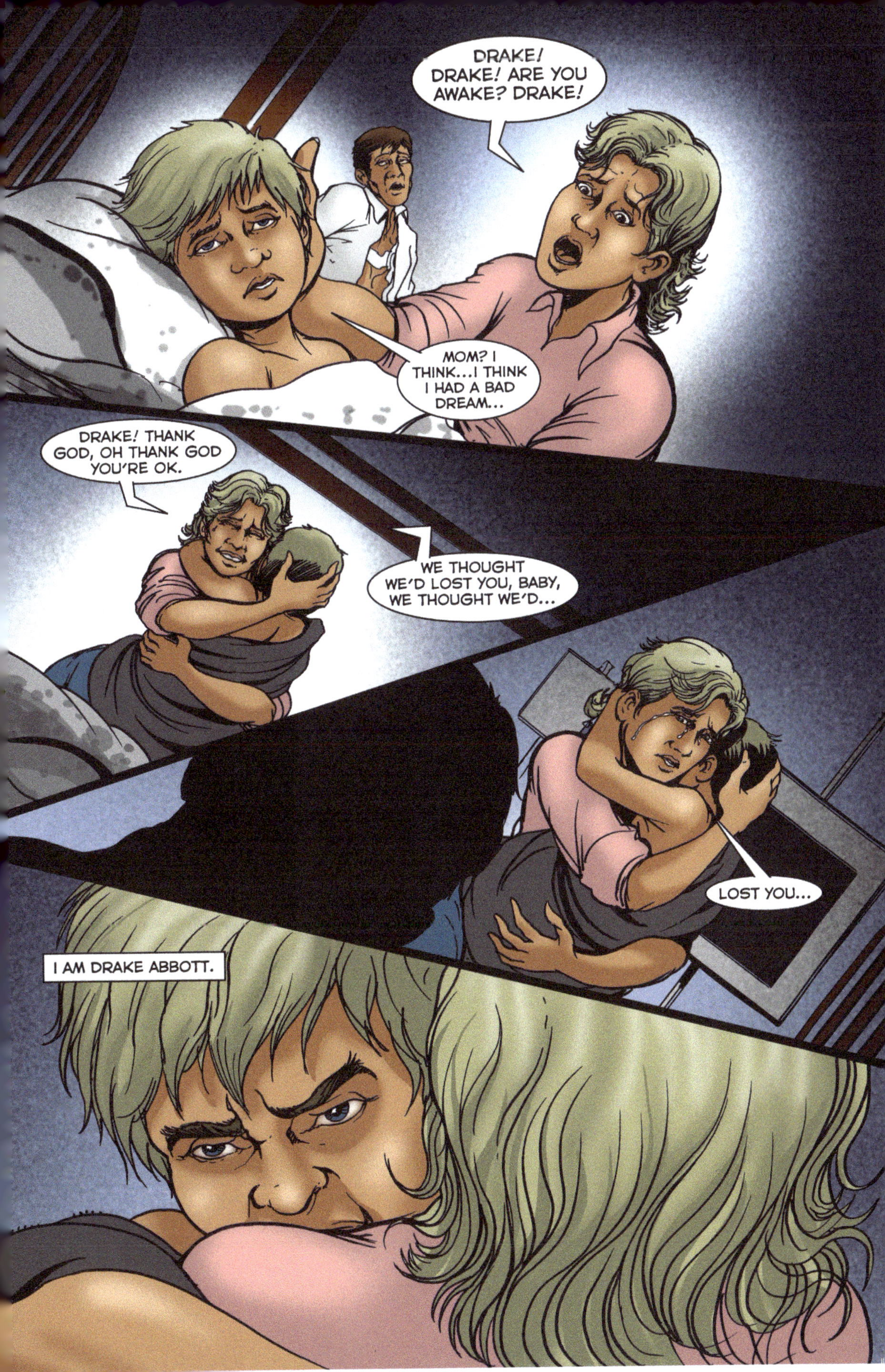
DRAKE! DRAKE! ARE YOU AWAKE? DRAKE!
MOM? I THINK...I THINK I HAD A BAD DREAM...
DRAKE! THANK GOD, OH THANK GOD YOU'RE OK.
WE THOUGHT WE'D LOST YOU, BABY, WE THOUGHT WE'D...
LOST YOU...
I AM DRAKE ABBOTT.

I HAVE FOUGHT CRIMINALS, AND MONSTERS.
I HAVE KNOWN THE LOVE OF GHOSTS AND MACHINES.
GO AND PLAY, BABY. IT'S OK.
I THINK YOUR CARTOONS ARE ON.
I HAVE WATCHED MY FATHER DIE.
DANIEL... OH DANIEL YOU IDIOT...
SHE WILL TELL HIM THAT IT WAS A BAD DREAM
JUST A STORY, NOTHING MORE
BUT SHE IS WRONG.

I AM DRAKE ABBOTT
AND I AM THE DARK.
END

LYNCH &
LUNDEEN
AAM/MARKOSIA

www.ingramcontent.com/pod-product-compliance
Ingram Content Group UK Ltd.
Pitfield, Milton Keynes, MK11 3LW, UK
UKHW061953290726
14090UKWH00021B/1202

9 781905 692378